Wild Fairies

Daisy's Decorating Dilemma

Written by Brandi Dougherty
Illustrated by Renée Kurilla

RODALE KiDS

For my wild fairies, Oslo and Charlie.
You inspire me every day!
—B.D.

For Eric.
Thanks so much for giving me the opportunity
to explore this new world!
—R.K.

Copyright © 2018 by Penguin Random House LLC

All rights reserved. Published in the United States by Rodale Kids,
an imprint of Random House Children's Books, a division of Penguin Random House LLC,
New York. Originally published in hardcover in the United States by Rodale Kids,
an imprint of Random House Children's Books, a division of
Penguin Random House LLC, New York, in 2018.

Rodale and the colophon are registered trademarks
and Rodale Kids is a trademark of Penguin Random House LLC.

Visit us on the Web! rhcbooks.com

Educators and librarians, for a variety of teaching tools, visit us at RHTeachersLibrarians.com

Library of Congress Cataloging-in-Publication Data is available upon request.
ISBN 978-1-63565-132-4 (trade) | ISBN 978-1-63565-133-1 (ebook) |
ISBN 978-1-63565-131-7 (pbk.)

MANUFACTURED IN CHINA
10 9 8 7 6 5 4 3 2 1
First Paperback Edition

Contents

Chapter 1

Daisy breathed in deep through her nose. Her wings fluttered in the soft breeze.

"Do you smell that?" she asked the other wild fairies as they hovered nearby. "Spring is in the air!" Daisy's blond curls bounced with her excitement. Her friend and sidekick, Bumble, whizzed in a circle around her. He was excited, too.

Spring was definitely in the air in Sugar Oak, the

fairies' grand oak tree home. Tiny buds of green were starting to appear at the ends of the old oak's branches. Birds were returning from their winter homes. They sang sweet songs to the fairies.

The wild fairies and their animal friends were very busy. It was time for the festival to celebrate the first bloom of spring. Blossom Bash was the biggest party of the year. This year it was the fairies' turn to host the festival. It was a big responsibility, and there were lots of things to prepare! Everybody was excited, especially Daisy.

Daisy was in charge of the festival preparations. It was her job to make sure that everyone had a task and that the tasks were completed in time. Daisy was a natural leader. And she loved helping her friends.

Poppy zoomed past Daisy and the other fairies. The red blooms of her dress flapped up and down as she flew by. Spot, Poppy's ladybug friend, beat her speckled wings, trying to keep up.

"Whoa!" said Thistle, as he somersaulted out of Poppy's way. Now his spiky purple hair stood up even more. "What's the hurry?"

"Fiddlesticks!" Poppy cried. "There's so much to do! I don't know how we're going to get ready in time!"

Daisy smiled at Poppy. She wasn't worried.
She was about to tell Poppy not to worry either
when a raindrop tickled the end of her nose.

Chapter 2

"Fiddlesticks!" Poppy cried again.

The wild fairies flitted into the Great Hall of Sugar Oak. They watched through the windows as the rain came down strong and hard. It was the first big rainstorm of the season.

"It's beautiful!" Celosia said. She wiggled her nose, and the freckles dotting her cheeks wiggled, too.

"All this rain will help the flowers grow. This is going to be the best spring bloom we've had in years!" Daisy added. She could already see the festival coming to life with colors everywhere.

"But we're not ready!" Poppy sighed. "The more rain we get, the sooner the bloom is going to happen."

"I didn't think about that," Indigo said. She
touched the purple bandana around her neck
and looked worried.

"What should we do?" Heather asked.

All the fairies looked at Daisy. She held up
her hands and smiled one of her warm, easy

smiles. "Everything is going to be fine!" she said. "We all have our jobs for the festival, so the work is being done. We just need to decide on decorations for Sugar Oak, and we have a meeting about that tonight."

"Do you have a to-do list?" Poppy asked. "What about a clipboard?"

Daisy laughed. "I don't have a clipboard, Poppy. And the plans are all up here." She tapped the side of her head, making the daisy flower in her hair jiggle.

Poppy frowned and plopped down on a tree knot. She was such a worrier!

Daisy flew over and gave her a quick hug. "It's going to be great. I promise!"

Chapter 3

That afternoon, the sun came out. It warmed the oak tree down to its roots. The wild fairies played a game of hide-and-seek. Then they drank honey lemonade and let the gentle spring sun warm their cheeks.

That evening after dinner, Daisy called their meeting to order at the edge of the pond so Lily could stay longer. Lily was a mermaid

and a wild fairy! She always had to leave
early because she could be out of the water for
only a little while.

Daisy cleared her throat. The fairies
quieted down. "Let's talk about the Blossom
Bash decorations for Sugar Oak," she started.
"How do we want to decorate the tree for the
festival?"

Everybody started talking all at once.

"I think we should use different shades of pink," Heather said. She smoothed her hand down her long, bright-pink hair.

"Thistle flowers are always nice," Thistle added.

Dahlia twirled in a circle, making her reddish-orange pigtails bounce. "Don't forget dahlias!" she said. "There are so many colors to choose from."

"We definitely need lots of red," Poppy said, smiling.

Daisy tried to write down everyone's suggestions. She had trouble keeping up! Every fairy had her or his own idea about how to decorate their home for the Blossom Bash.

"Maybe we should vote," Lily suggested.

Daisy looked at the list. "But there are seven ideas here and seven of you!"

"True," Indigo laughed. "We all like our
own idea best!"

The wild fairies giggled and nodded. Daisy
gave a small smile. But she was a little nervous.
How would she ever decide which idea
to choose?

Thistle

Dahlia

Heather

Poppy

Indigo

Celosia

Daisy

Water Lily

Chapter 4

That night, Daisy sat on the bed in her nook with Bumble. She looked at her notes from the meeting. Everyone had such great ideas for decorating the tree. And Daisy wanted to make them all happy. She just wasn't sure how!

"Decorating Sugar Oak is a big job," Daisy told Bumble. "I know it would look beautiful with any of these themes. And, of course, I thought daisies would be perfect decorations, too..."

*Pink
*Thistle
*Dahlias
*Lots of RED!!!

Bumble buzzed in agreement.

Daisy thought about last year's festival. The bugs in Golden Meadow had hosted the party. They wove baskets out of grass and filled them with flower blossoms.

And the year before that, the birds of Cottonwood hosted. They hung puffs of cotton that looked like clouds floating all around them. Daisy wanted their party to be just as good as—if not better than—the other festivals!

Just then, Daisy heard a sound. She moved to the window and peeked out. The moon was hidden in the clouds. There was that sound again. She stuck her hand out the window. Drip, drop, SPLAT. Raindrops pattered her hand.

Poppy's words floated through Daisy's mind. *The more rain we get, the sooner the bloom is going to happen!*

Daisy shook her blond curls and looked at Bumble. "Everything's going to be fine!" she said. But her smile disappeared when the rain came down even harder. What if Poppy was right?

Chapter 5

The next morning, Daisy peeked out her window and beamed. "There are almost no clouds in the sky!" she told Bumble. "No clouds means no rain."

Bumble made a happy buzzing sound.

Daisy decided she would check in with each of her fairy friends to see how their festival jobs were going. She wanted to lend a hand wherever she could.

She flew out her door and almost ran right into Thistle.

"Hey there—*ahchoo!*—Daisy," Thistle said. "I was coming to—*ahchoo!*—talk to you."

"Good morning, Thistle," Daisy laughed. Poor Thistle always had allergies in the spring. As soon as the trees started to blossom and pollen began to float in the air, Thistle began to sneeze. Daisy patted her friend on the shoulder. "I have just the thing for your..."

AH...AH...AHCHOO! Thistle flew backward with the force of his sneeze. He knocked into a tree branch. His beetle friend, Spike, jumped out of the way.

Daisy darted into her nook and returned with a small jar.

Thistle peered into the jar. "Honey?"

Daisy beamed. "Honey is great for allergies. Just take a little spoonful each morning, and you'll feel better in no time."

"Thank you, Daisy!" Thistle said, dipping his finger into the jar. "Mmmmm."

"So, what did you want to talk to me about?" Daisy asked as they flew.

"Have you made a decision about the festival decorations yet?" Thistle asked.

"Not yet," said Daisy. "But I will soon! How are the plans for the parade coming along?"

"Great! The floats are almost done. I just can't decide what kind of leaves to use for the base of the forest float."

"Hmmm." Daisy thought for a minute. "What about maple leaves?"

"Yes! That's perfect," said Thistle. "Thanks!"

"Anytime!"

AHCHOO!

Just then Poppy flew by. "Your allergies are starting, Thistle?" she asked. "You know what that means, don't you?"

Poppy's eyes were wide. "It means flowers are already blooming! We aren't ready!"

Daisy knew Poppy was right, but she kept her smile firmly in place. "We'll be fine!" she said.

Chapter 6

$\mathcal{D}$aisy and Bumble made their way to the Great Hall. Daisy needed to check in with Heather about the food preparations for the festival. She knew everything would be fine, but Poppy was starting to make her a teeny bit nervous!

They found Heather and her butterfly friend, Flutter, in the kitchen. Heather wore a light-pink apron over her flowing pink dress. She was stirring something over the fire. It bubbled and gurgled in the pot. And it smelled amazing!

"Hi, Heather!" Daisy said brightly. "How is the food for Blossom Bash coming along?"

Heather smiled wide. "Come taste for yourself!" she said. She dipped a wooden spoon into the pot and held it out for Daisy. Daisy slurped it up right away.

She closed her eyes and smiled. "That's the yummiest!"

"It's a new recipe: hazelnut stew!"

"I love it," Daisy said. She looked around the kitchen. There were fruits and vegetables, herbs and nuts, and flowers and plants covering every surface. "Looks like you have lots to work with!"

"Yes!" Heather said. "We'll have plenty of food for everyone."

"Is there anything I can help you with?" Daisy asked.

"Yes, one thing," Heather replied. "Do you think I should make honey cakes or nectar cookies?"

"Definitely honey cakes!" Daisy said right away.

"Great! By the way, have you made a decision about the decorations yet?"

"Not yet," Daisy replied. "But soon."

"Because pink really is the perfect color for welcoming spring," Heather said. Flutter flapped her pink wings and flew in a circle around Daisy and Bumble.

Daisy laughed at Flutter. She could
imagine Sugar Oak covered in shades of pink.
It would be lovely. But what about the other
wild fairies' ideas?

Chapter 7

$\mathcal{N}$ext, Daisy and Bumble flitted down to the pond. Daisy wanted to see how Celosia and Lily were doing. They were in charge of the entertainment. Daisy could hear Celosia's beautiful voice floating up on the breeze.

Daisy sat down on a log to watch. Celosia and her friend Chirp were singing. Lily's friend Splash and the other frogs provided backup music. Lily bobbed and dipped in the water. Her blue hair skimmed the surface of the pond. Her lily pad wings beat in time to the music. At

the end of the song, she flipped her tail fin into the air. She was very graceful.

Daisy clapped and cheered. "That was wonderful!"

"Daisy!" Lily cried. "We didn't see you there!"

"I came to see how the entertainment was coming along for Blossom Bash. It looks like you are more than ready!"

"We've been practicing a lot," Celosia said.

"I can tell," Daisy replied. "Do you need help with anything?"

Lily swam over to the edge of the pond. "Maybe you *can* help us with something. We're trying to decide between 'Spring Has Sprung' and 'Bloom Boogie Oogie' as the final song."

"I say 'Bloom Boogie Oogie,'" Daisy replied.

"It's so fun. I know everyone will dance and sing along."

"Good point. Thanks, Daisy!" Celosia said.

"Have you picked the Sugar Oak decorations yet?" Lily asked hopefully.

"Not yet," Daisy said.

"You got my idea, right? About the lilies?"
Lily asked.

Daisy smiled. "I did! I got Celosia's idea,
too. They're both great."

"Okay, just making sure." With that, Lily
did a dramatic dive into the water and surfaced
next to Splash, who croaked in surprise.

Daisy, Celosia, and Lily all laughed.

Daisy stood up and dusted off her white dress. "See you all later!"

"Don't forget about lilies!" Lily shouted after her.

Chapter 8

*L*ater that afternoon, the sun began to dip behind the trees. More clouds appeared in the sky. Daisy headed back to her nook to think about the plan for decorations. She still didn't know what she was going to do! She arrived to find Poppy pacing back and forth outside her door.

"There you are!" Poppy said, throwing her hands in the air. "I've been looking all over for you!"

"Hi, Poppy. What's up?" Daisy asked as Bumble and Spot said hello.

"Did you make a decision yet?"

Daisy shook her head. "No, not yet. I've been busy with other things." Daisy thought about how she had spent the day checking in with the other fairies on their projects.

"Fiddlesticks!" Poppy cried. "I'm just so worried!"

Just then, Dahlia bounded up beside them on the back of her squirrel sidekick, Peanut.

"Worried about what?" Dahlia asked.

"Poppy is worried that we won't be ready for Blossom Bash before the first bloom of spring," Daisy explained. "And I still haven't chosen the decorations..."

Dahlia hopped off Peanut's back and took a sip of flower nectar from a small bottle she carried. "Blossom Bash is going to be great!"

she said. "Everything will work out. You'll see!"

Daisy smiled gratefully. She needed some of Dahlia's optimism. Dahlia never got upset about anything!

"You're in charge of making sure we have enough tables and chairs for the banquet, right?" Daisy asked Poppy. "How's that going?"

"Everything's ready. We'll have plenty of space for everyone," Poppy replied. "I just need to decide what to use for umbrellas to shade the tables from the sun."

Daisy thought for a minute.

"Chrysanthemums make nice shady umbrellas. And they're pretty, too!"

"That's a great idea," Poppy said. "Thanks, Daisy!"

"Daisy, you've been helping everyone else make decisions for Blossom Bash," Dahlia said. "Be sure to ask for help for yourself, too!"

"I will. I..."

Just then, a fat raindrop, followed by another and then another, bounced off Daisy's curls.

Chapter 9

$\mathcal{D}$aisy and Bumble quickly said goodbye to Dahlia and Poppy. They darted through the branches to the top of the oak. They tried to stay out of the rain on their way to Indigo's workshop. Daisy knew she was working on a special project for Blossom Bash and wanted to see how things were going.

When they reached the workshop, Daisy heard lots of banging and clanging inside.

"Hello?" she called.

"Back here!" Indigo shouted.

Daisy stepped inside and shook the rain from her dress. She made her way through a maze of baskets, tools, and trinkets of all shapes and sizes.

"Hey!" Indigo popped up from under her worktable.

"What are you working on?" Daisy asked. She looked at all the wonderful things covering the table. There were seashells and sea glass, acorns and walnut shells, and dried leaves and flowers.

Indigo blew her hair out of her eyes and smiled. The purple streak in front flapped back in front of her eyes. She nodded toward her caterpillar friend, Fuzz. "We've been

collecting things from all around Sugar Oak
and the whole forest. We're stringing the pieces
together so we can hang them above the tables
at Blossom Bash."

Daisy was quiet.

"I know you haven't chosen the decorations
yet," Indigo said quickly. "But I figured this
would fit in somehow..."

Slowly, Daisy's mouth turned up into a smile. She pulled Indigo in for a big hug.

"What was that for?" Indigo asked.

"You just gave me an idea!" Daisy responded. Then she was off like a flash.

Chapter 10

When the wild fairies met at the pond later that evening, Daisy couldn't stay still. She was so excited to reveal the decoration plans for Blossom Bash. Finally, all the fairies and their animal friends arrived.

"I know how we're going to decorate Sugar Oak for the festival," Daisy began. They waited in anticipation. "We're going to use everyone's ideas!"

None of the fairies spoke.

"But how?" Poppy finally asked.

"Instead of using one theme for the entire festival, each of you can choose something to decorate. And you can use whatever materials, colors, and designs you like! That way, we will all see something of ourselves in the party."

"That's a great idea, Daisy!" Dahlia said. All the wild fairies agreed.

"I have to thank Indigo for helping me come up with it," Daisy replied. She was about to say something else when lightning flashed across the darkening sky. It was followed by a loud clap of thunder.

"Fiddlesticks!" Poppy cried. The other fairies froze and looked at each other. Everyone was starting to get nervous about the rain, not just Poppy.

Daisy felt herself getting nervous, too. But then she thought about how hard she and her friends had been working. And Dahlia was right—everything was going to work out.

"Even if the flowers bloom before Blossom Bash begins, it's going to be great!" Daisy told her friends. "We all know we can't control nature. We can only appreciate all that it gives us. And that's what this celebration is really about!"

The fairies cheered. Daisy smiled at each of her friends. She couldn't wait to see what they came up with.

Chapter 11

The fairies spent the next couple of days
finishing their preparations for Blossom
Bash. When a few flowers bloomed early,
nobody minded. They were having too much
fun decorating to worry! Indigo's strings of
sea glass and other trinkets hung above the
banquet tables like twinkly lights. A bright-
red poppy flower was fixed to the back of each
chair. Deep-purple thistle and celosia flowers
stood all along the parade route. Dahlias and
daisies were scattered across the path leading

to the pond. Airy sprigs of heather hung upside
down from Sugar Oak's branches. And lilies
floated in baskets at the edge of the water. It
was wonderful!

The day of Blossom Bash was the sunniest
spring day yet. Daisy put an extra flower in

her hair. The wild fairies' animal friends arrived from all around the forest. There were the bugs from Golden Meadow and the birds from Cottonwood. There were also chipmunks from Pine Cone Terrace, rabbits from Craggy Log, and turtles from Seashell Beach. It was a huge party!

The first event of the day was the Blossom Bash parade. Daisy was delighted to

see the work her friends had put into making the floats. When the flowers fell off one of the floats, Thistle started to get upset. But Daisy sprang into action. She picked up the fallen petals and sprinkled them over the parade like a shower of spring blossoms.

Next, the fairies had a delicious feast. The food Heather prepared was even better than

Daisy and the others imagined. They had fruit tarts, mushroom pie, nut casseroles, and berry juice teas. It was delicious. When they ran out of hazelnut stew, Heather was worried. But Daisy just gave everyone an extra honey cake.

Then it was time for the entertainment. Celosia's song and Lily's dance had everyone

clapping and cheering. When one of the backup frogs lost her voice, Daisy jumped in to sing along.

As the sun went down, the fireflies created a light display over the pond. Their lights twinkled and danced in the twilight like tiny sparks. It was beautiful. For the grand finale, the fairies and their animal friends danced to the "Bloom Boogie Oogie." Blossom Bash was a

"The Sugar Oak decorations are spectacular!" one of the rabbits told Daisy as they danced.

"Thank you!" Daisy beamed.

Before everyone headed home full and happy, the wild fairies presented Daisy with a special Blossom Bash award.

"This is for being so helpful to everyone," Heather explained. "Blossom Bash came together because of you!"

Daisy happily accepted her award but held up her hand to quiet the crowd. "Blossom Bash was great because we all worked together. I couldn't have done it without all my wild fairy friends!" she said. Everyone clapped and cheered.

Daisy couldn't have been happier. "I had the best time!" she told Poppy as they flew home to their nooks.

"Even though the festival wasn't *totally* perfect?" Poppy asked.

Daisy smiled. "Sometimes special is even better than perfect. And today was an extra-special day."

All About Honey

Honey is an amazing natural substance made by—you guessed it—honeybees! First, the bees gather nectar from inside flower blossoms. Then, the nectar is passed from bee to bee and eventually deposited in honeycomb. Finally, bees use their wings to fan the honey and make it thicker. Honey is naturally delicious, and it's also good for you!

If you have seasonal allergies, like Thistle does, honey can help you feel better. Because honey is collected from flowers, a little bit of flower pollen is included in honey. Pollen is what most people with allergies are allergic to. So, by eating a tiny bit of pollen found in honey, your body can help build up an immunity to the flower that makes you sneeze! Just be sure the honey you eat is local to your area so that it includes pollen from flowers near your home. You can find local honey at the farmer's market!

Honey is also great for boosting your energy or soothing your throat when you have a cough. The honey acts like a nice warm coat that keeps your throat from getting irritated and dry. You can even use honey if you get a scrape or a cut—just dab a little bit right on your wound and the honey will help to keep it clean.

Isn't honey sweet?

To encourage bees to make honey in your neighborhood, you can plant some flowers and trees that bees like, such as sunflowers, lavender, and goldenrod. Then they will have all the nectar they need!

Heather's Honey Cakes

Yield: About 24 cupcakes

These sweet treats are Daisy's favorite! They're great for any occasion, not just the Blossom Bash. Top them with your favorite fresh fruit to make them even yummier!

1/2 cup butter, softened

3 large eggs

1 cup sugar

1 cup honey

1 teaspoon baking powder

Juice of 1 lemon

3/4 cup milk

1 teaspoon baking soda

2 cups flour

Fresh fruit, optional

1. With a grownup's supervision, preheat the oven to 350°F.

2. In a large bowl, cream together the butter, sugar, and eggs using a hand or stand mixer.

3. Mix in the honey, baking powder, lemon juice, and milk. Then add the baking soda and flour, and mix until fully incorporated.

4. Line a cupcake tin with cupcake liners, and then spoon the batter into the liners until they are two-thirds full.

5. Bake for 15 minutes, or until a toothpick inserted in the middle comes out clean, then let cool on a wire rack.

6. Enjoy plain or topped with your favorite fresh fruit, if you wish!

Meet the Wild Fairies!

Get to know the wild fairies
and their critter companions a little
bit better! Read on to find out
more about each friend.

Daisy

Daisy is a natural leader, and she's lots of fun to be around. She has a bubbly personality and a great laugh. The other wild fairies often look to Daisy to guide them through tricky situations.

Likes: Big dinners in the Great Hall with all her friends
Dislikes: Getting dirty
Favorite activity: Party planning
Favorite food: Honey cakes (yum!)
Favorite color: Green
Favorite season: All of them!

Fun fact: Even though Daisy doesn't like to get dirty, she is such a good friend that she once dug in the mud to help Indigo look for a tool she had dropped!

Bumble

Bumble the bumblebee is Daisy's sweet sidekick. Bumble is a great listener and is there for Daisy whenever she needs him.

Poppy

Poppy is a planner! She likes to organize everything to make sure it's just right. But that also means Poppy can be a little stressed out sometimes.

Likes: Making lists
Dislikes: Change
Favorite activity: Playing hide-and-seek or tag
Favorite food: Strawberries
Favorite color: Red, of course!
Favorite season: Summer

Fun fact: Whenever Poppy gets worried about something, she says, "Fiddlesticks!"

Spot

Poppy's friend Spot is a ladybug with bright red wings. She tries very hard to keep Poppy's worry in check and is always there to make her feel calm and happy.

Thistle

Despite his spiky hair and wings, Thistle is very warm and friendly. He's always looking out for others and likes to stay close to his friends in case they need help.

Likes: Telling stories in the Great Hall
Dislikes: Having allergies
Favorite activity: Visiting Pine Cone Terrace
Favorite food: Hazelnut stew
Favorite color: Gray
Favorite season: Winter (there's no pollen in winter!)

Fun fact: Thistle once rescued a baby chipmunk from a pesky raccoon. The chipmunk's family still invites Thistle to dinner!

Spike

Thistle and Spike the beetle go everywhere together. The wild fairies can always count on them for a good story. Spike likes to be silly and makes a great comedy team with Thistle!

Dahlia

Dahlia has an adventurous spirit. She likes to try new things and doesn't get worried about much— she knows things will work out!

Likes: Surprises!
Dislikes: When a friend is sad or upset
Favorite activity: Exploring new places
Favorite food: Apples
Favorite color: Orange
Favorite season: Fall

Fun fact: Dahlia loves surprises, but she's terrible at keeping secrets! She accidentally spilled the beans about Thistle's surprise birthday party.

Peanut

Peanut is a red squirrel, and he's just as adventurous as Dahlia. Peanut is a big help carrying supplies or pulling a wagon for building projects.

Heather

Heather's heart is as big as her bright pink hair. She's an amazing cook, and she's also great at coming up with herbal remedies when a fairy feels sick.

Likes: Taking care of her fairy friends
Dislikes: Running low on supplies
Favorite activity: Baking
Favorite food: It's too hard to pick just one!
Favorite color: Pink
Favorite season: Fall

Fun fact: Heather is so in tune with nature that she can sniff out hidden herbs and flowers with her nose!

Flutter

Flutter is a beautiful pink butterfly. She's a whiz at helping Heather in the kitchen. She picks up herbs and spices and drops them in the pot for Heather while she's cooking! Much like Heather's nose, Flutter's antennae are great at finding hidden treats!

Indigo

Indigo is fearless and creative. She spends equal amounts of time creating things in her workshop and exploring the forest. The other wild fairies come to Indigo when they need help solving a problem. She has a unique way of looking at things.

Likes: Challenges!
Dislikes: Being told "no!"
Favorite activity: Inventing things
Favorite food: Fig jam tarts
Favorite color: Purple
Favorite season: Winter

Fun fact: When Indigo injured her wing, she made a glider to help her sail down Sugar Oak to the pond!

Fuzz

Fuzz the caterpillar is a handy helper in Indigo's workshop with lots of hands for holding tools! Fuzz is pretty quiet, but he is sure to let Indigo know when he likes one of her new ideas.

Celosia

Celosia is a talented poet and musician. She has a bright smile and a beautiful voice. She loves to use her music to make her friends happy.

Likes: Writing poems and songs
Dislikes: Gray, dreary weather
Favorite activity: Singing!
Favorite food: Pomegranate puffs
Favorite color: Yellow
Favorite season: Spring

Fun fact: Celosia's Sugar Oak home inspires her to write something new almost every single day.

Chirp

Chirp the sparrow is the perfect companion for a singer like Celosia. Chirp has a lovely singing voice of her own and is happy to provide backup vocals for all of Celosia's songs.

Lily

Lily is a mermaid wild fairy who likes to make a splash! She can be very dramatic and loves to show off a new water dance routine.

Likes: Water ballet
Dislikes: Feeling bored
Favorite activity: Performing
Favorite food: Kelp cupcakes
Favorite color: Blue
Favorite season: Spring

Fun fact: Lily has worked hard to perfect a very difficult stunt. She can now launch herself out of the water and twirl in a perfect circle!

Splash

Splash is a frog and Lily's best friend. They have hours of fun together—from playing games in the pond to eating lunch together in Lily's cozy cottage.

Meet the Author

BRANDI DOUGHERTY is the author of the *New York Times* bestselling picture book *The Littlest Pilgrim* along with six other Littlest tales. She's also written three middle-grade novels, a Pixar picture book, and four books in Giada De Laurentiis's Recipe for Adventure series. She lives in Los Angeles, where she wrangles two adorable kids and one crazy dog with her husband, Joe. Visit brandidougherty.com.

Meet the Illustrator

RENÉE KURILLA has illustrated many books for kids, including *Orangutanka* by Margarita Engle and *The Pickwicks' Picnic* by Carol Brendler. She lives in the woods just south of Boston—the perfect place to search for wild fairies! Visit kurillastration.com.

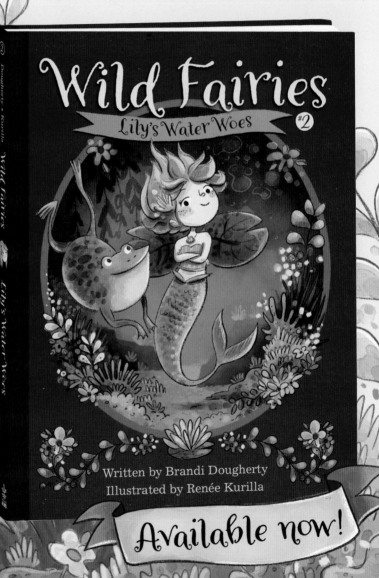